Books by Robert Bright

The Friendly Bear
Georgie
Georgie's Halloween
Georgie to the Rescue
I Like Red
Me and the Bears
Richard Brown and the Dragon
Georgie and the Magician
Georgie and the Robbers
Which is Willy?

Georgie's Halloween

written and illustrated by Robert Bright

Doubleday and Company, Inc., Garden City, New York

ISBN: 0-385-07773-4 TRADE
0-385-07778-5 PREBOUND
Copyright © 1958 by Robert Bright
Library of Congress Catalog Card Number 58-7154
Lithographed in the United States of America
All Rights Reserved.

15   14   13   12   11   10

Wherever there are children there is Halloween, with pumpkins and funny faces, with tricks and with treats. But in the little village where Mr. and Mrs. Whittaker lived there was always something extra besides, and that was Georgie, the little ghost who lived in the Whittaker attic.

Every Halloween while the children went trick or treating—blowing horns, banging dishpans, making all the LOUD NOISES—Georgie went a-haunting with his friends, Herman the cat and Miss Oliver the owl.

But while the children rang doorbells
and shouted boldly for treats, Georgie
stayed hidden, and maybe you saw him
—just maybe—and maybe you didn't.

And that was just as it should be, because Georgie was a gentle little ghost
and he was shy.

Now everything would have gone on just as usual year after year, except that one Halloween was different. That was the time they had a notion to give a big party for all the children on the Village Green, and Mr. Whittaker himself was chosen to present the prize for the best Halloween costume.

That Halloween everybody dressed up "special."
Herman did——
Miss Oliver did——

Mr. and Mrs. Whittaker did, and rode to the Green in style.

Everybody dressed up "special" except Georgie, because Georgie didn't have to. He was so especially perfect for Halloween just as he was. It just didn't seem proper that Georgie shouldn't go to the party and win the prize!

All the mice in the attic thought he should——

Herman thought so—
Miss Oliver did,
and they called
to Georgie.

The pumpkin in the parlor window grinned at Georgie—
The Halloween moon in the sky smiled at him.

But while Georgie went to the party on the Green and saw the apple-bobbing and pinning the tail on the donkey, he stayed hidden,

and maybe you saw him—
just maybe—and maybe you didn't.

And when it was time for the prize contest to begin, and the children crowded around the bandstand, Georgie wasn't anywhere near enough.

Just the same he was curious
and it did seem like such fun.
Besides, Herman and Miss Oliver
urged him on—
and so, presently, he did come nearer—

and a little nearer—

until he was
right behind
a corn shock
that decorated
the bandstand,
where he had
the best kind of view.

That seemed plenty good enough for Georgie, except that Herman kept meowing at him so, and Miss Oliver kept whoo-whooing at him so—urging him to be brave.

And so Georgie screwed up every bit of courage he had.

Now Mr. Whittaker did not see him even then, he was so busy looking the wrong way. But the children saw him and recognized their favorite little ghost. And so they shouted all together: "It's Georgie! It's GEORGIE!"

If only they had not shouted quite so loud!

Or if only Mr. Whittaker had looked around a little quicker. Because he could have sworn that — somebody — SOMEBODY — had tugged at his coattail. But Georgie was gone in a second.

Georgie was running home lickety-split to tell the mice
in the attic about it, and all the way he could still hear
the children cheering him.

Now the mice understood why
Georgie ran lickety-split
back to the attic.
Because they were so shy
themselves.

They had a special
surprise for Georgie.

And maybe it was the best kind of prize for Halloween because it had come right out of a very old creaky and squeaky bureau drawer.

At that, Georgie was so happy and pleased, he might well have forgotten everything else. But even tonight, as soon as Mr. and Mrs. Whittaker were home again—

Georgie did not forget
to creak the stairs,
just as usual—

or to squeak the parlor door, just as usual.

And Herman did not forget to prowl after his favorite mouse, and Miss Oliver did not forget to sing her owl song, just as she always did in her favorite tree.

As for Mr. and Mrs. Whittaker, they were still so puzzled and betwizzled by what had happened on the Green that, while they went to bed as they should, they forgot to blow out the pumpkin in the parlor window.

But Georgie took care of that, thank goodness!